CURIOUS CATS

ALVIN SILVERSTEIN · VIRGINIA SILVERSTEIN · LAURA SILVERSTEIN NUNN

TWENTY-FIRST CENTURY BOOKS
BROOKFIELD, CONNECTICUT

Cover photograph courtesy of Photo Researchers, Inc. (© Jane Howard)
Photographs courtesy of © Chanan Photo: pp. 6, 14, 18; Photo Researchers, Inc.: pp. 10 (© Carolyn A. McKeone), 34 (© M. Austin), 42 (© Terry Whittaker); © SuperStock: p. 22; Animals Animals: pp. 26 (© Ralph Reinhold), 30 (© Werner Layer), 38 (© Henry Ausloos)

Library of Congress Cataloging-in-Publication Data
Silverstein, Alvin.
Curious cats / by Alvin & Virginia Silverstein & Laura Silverstein Nunn.
p. cm. — (What a pet!)
Summary: Introduces ten unusual breeds of cats and offers advice on their care, feeding, and breeding.
ISBN 0-7613-2512-3 (lib. bdg.)
1. Cats—Juvenile literature. 2. Cat breeds—Juvenile literature.
[1. Cats. 2. Cat breeds. 3. Pets.] I. Silverstein, Virginia B. II. Nunn, Laura Silverstein. III. Title. IV. Series: Silverstein, Alvin. What a pet!
SF445.7.S573 2003
636.8—dc21
2002154609

Published by Twenty-First Century Books
A Division of The Millbrook Press, Inc.
2 Old New Milford Road
Brookfield, CT 06804
www.millbrookpress.com

CONTENTS

Cat Breeds

Most domestic cat breeds recognized today are less than a century old, although a few breeds date back hundreds or even thousands of years. New breeds are still being developed, and some win acceptance by local and national cat-breeding associations such as the Cat Fanciers' Association (CFA) and The Independent Cat Association (TICA). Breeders carefully select matings to establish traits such as:

coat color and markings: tabby (striped or spotted, like the domestic cat's wild ancestors); solid-colored (which usually show a faint tabby pattern in bright light); all-white cats; piebald (a color with various amounts of white, such as "mittens" or most of the body); tortoiseshell (both black and red hair) and calico (tortoiseshell with patches of white); and pointed (cream or tan coat with colored hairs on ears, muzzle, paws, and tail)

hair length: longhaired (such as Persian and Angora) and shorthaired (such as Siamese, Abyssinian, and "domestic shorthairs"); about 90 percent of pet cats are mixed-breed domestic shorthairs, although they may carry longhair genes

body type: cobby (short-bodied, heavy-boned, such as Manx); Oriental (long, slender body and legs, and fine bones, such as Siamese); and intermediate (most domestic cats)

head shape: round (such as Scottish fold), rectangle (most cats), and wedge (Oriental)

eye shape: round, oval, and almond (a slanted, narrow oval)

WHAT A PET!

THIS SERIES WILL GIVE you information about some well-known animals and some unusual ones. It will help you to select a pet suitable for your family and for where you live. It will also tell you about animals that should not be pets. It is important for you to understand that many people who work with animals are strongly opposed to keeping *any* wild creature as a pet.

People tend to want to keep exotic animals. But they forget that often it is illegal to have them as pets or that they require a great deal of special care and will never really become good pets. A current fad of owning an exotic animal may quickly pass, and the animals suffer. Their owners may abandon them in an effort to return them to the wild, even though the animals can no longer survive there. Or they may languish in small cages without proper food and exercise.

Before selecting any animal as a pet, it is a good idea to learn as much as you can about it. This series will help you, and your local veterinarian and the ASPCA are good sources of information. You should also find out if it is endangered. Phone numbers for each state wildlife agency can be found on the Internet at

www.rzu2u.com/states.htm

Any pet is a big responsibility—your responsibility. The most important thing to keep in mind when selecting a pet is the welfare of the animal.

F A S T   F A C T S

Scientific name	*Felis catus* in Family Felidae, Order Carnivora
Cost	About $300 to $400
Food	Commercial cat food, water
Housing	Can be kept indoors or outdoors. Needs plenty of room to roam, so a small apartment may not be suitable for this active breed. Indoors, the cat may use a cat bed but will sleep anywhere it pleases. Provide cat toys to keep it busy and entertained; also a scratching post for sharpening its claws, otherwise it may damage the furniture.
Training	Training requires patience. Most cats can be easily trained to use a litter box. A cat can learn to respond to its name (although it may not always come when you call it). Some cats can be trained to walk on a leash. Some can even learn to do tricks, such as shaking hands (paws) and retrieving a toy. Treats are helpful in teaching tricks.
Special notes	Since Abys are energetic with a muscular build, it is important that they get plenty of exercise. Indoor "trees" or other cat-friendly objects can be used for climbing. This active breed needs enough food to fuel its high energy level.

ABYSSINIAN

ABYSSINIAN CATS LOOK amazingly similar to the elegant cats in ancient Egyptian drawings and sculptures. Some people think that Abyssinians are actually direct descendants of these ancient cats. There is no real evidence for this, however.

Today's Abyssinians, commonly called Abys, are long-legged animals, with a slender but muscular body. Their sleek, short-haired coats are often a reddish tan, with a subtle blending of other colors. They look very much like the African wildcats that were the ancestors of the first domestic cats.

THE ORIGIN OF THE ABYSSINIAN

While it may look like the descendant of an ancient Egyptian cat, today's Abyssinian actually dates back no further than the nineteenth century. The first Abyssinian cats, including one known as Zula, were brought to Britain in 1868 by British soldiers returning from Abyssinia (now Ethiopia) after the Abyssinian War. Zula may or may not have been the ancestor of today's Abys, but her attractive appearance set the standard for the Abyssinian we know today.

The Abyssinian was not recognized as a separate breed until 1882. But in 1887 when the National Cat Society was established, the name Abyssinian was dropped. Instead they called it the British ticked, bunny, or hare cat because the cat's ticked, agouti fur looked like that of a wild rabbit. (A ticked, agouti coat is one in which each individual hair is made up of bands of light and dark colors that gives a blended appearance.)

> **DID YOU KNOW?**
> Cats were the last of the domestic animals to be tamed—and perhaps their independent personalities are an indication that cats are not yet as completely tamed as dogs, horses, or cattle.

The name Abyssinian was reestablished in 1929, when the Abyssinian Cat Club was formed in England. Abyssinians were first brought to the United States during the 1930s, and breeding programs began shortly thereafter. Today, the Aby is the fourth most popular cat breed in the United States.

The First House Cats

The first house cats lived in Egypt about five thousand years ago. They are thought to have been bred from local African wildcats, some of which probably invited themselves into people's homes and farms after the Egyptians started to plant and store grain and other crops that attracted rodent pests. The cats helped to keep the pests under control. Even today, African wildcats are easily tamed and breed freely with domestic cats; their offspring are also mild-tempered and make good house cats.

Egyptian records dating back to 3500 B.C. show pictures of cats hunting with their masters and living in temples and houses. The ancient Egyptians worshiped their cats and treated them like royalty. In fact, the penalty for killing a cat in ancient Egypt was death! There were special cat cemeteries, and many cats were mummified just like the pharaohs.

For thousands of years cats were not very common elsewhere. In the first century B.C., in the time of Caesar and Cleopatra, the Romans conquered Egypt and took some cats back home with them. Soon cats were common in Rome. Then the Roman armies took cats along with them as they conquered Europe and Britain.

During the Middle Ages (from A.D. 500 to about 1500), cats were considered evil and thought to possess powers of black magic. Thousands of cats in Europe were hunted and killed. As their numbers dwindled, the rat population increased, which led to the spread of plagues and other epidemics throughout Europe.

By the seventeenth century cats once again lived peacefully with humans and kept the rodent population under control. Cats with an unusual color or body shape were prized and were used to produce separate breeds. By the late 1800s, the first cat shows were held in England and the United States.

ABYSSINIANS AS PETS

The Abyssinian is a medium-sized cat with a strong, muscular body. It is best known for its sleek, ticked agouti coat all over its body, except for the face, which has a tabby face mask. (The term *tabby* usually refers to a striped coat.) Originally, the only acceptable color for the Abyssinian agouti coat was ruddy brown (reddish brown ticked with black). Several other colors are now recognized in the breed: sorrel (copper-red with red-brown ticking), blue (blue-gray with dark gray ticking), beige-fawn (yellowish brown with cream ticking), and silver (silver-white with one of various ticking colors, including black, blue, sorrel, or beige-fawn).

Abyssinians are very affectionate, but they are *not* lap cats. They would rather be around you than be picked up or cuddled. Abys are very curious and love to investigate anything that piques their interest. They may try to open up drawers or cabinets to find out what's inside. These cats are very active and need lots of attention. Abyssinians like to be in high places, such as on a refrigerator or a bookshelf. So it is not a good idea to keep breakable objects out in the open. Owners say that the Abyssinian has a Peter Pan personality—it is a bundle of energy well into adulthood.

INTERNET RESOURCES

www.cfainc.org/breeds/profiles/abyssinian.html
"CFA Breed Profile: Abyssinian"

www.tdl.com/~pattic/abyfaq/ "Abyssinian FAQ"

www.cfainc.org/breeds/profiles/somali.html "CFA Breed Profile: Somali"

www.fanciers.com/breed-faqs/somali-faq.html "Somali: Cat Breed FAQ"

Longhaired Abys

During the 1950s, breeders were surprised when longhaired kittens started appearing in Abyssinian litters. Breeders considered longhaired Abyssinians nonstandard and unacceptable, and they quietly got rid of them. It wasn't until the 1960s that breeders realized the beauty of this longhaired version, which quickly gained popularity in the United States. To distinguish this breed from the shorthaired Abyssinian, it was named Somali, after Somalia, the country that borders Ethiopia (formerly Abyssinia). In 1972, the Somali Cat Club was established, and the Somali became an officially recognized breed. Today, the Somali is a greatly admired breed and a champion at cat shows.

FAST FACTS

Scientific name	*Felis catus* in Family Felidae, Order Carnivora
Cost	$300 to $1,200 (more for show quality)
Food	Commercial cat food, water
Housing	Can be kept indoors or outdoors. Needs plenty of room to roam, so a small apartment may not be suitable for this active breed. Indoors, the cat may use a cat bed but will sleep anywhere it pleases. Provide cat toys to keep it busy and entertained; also a scratching post for sharpening its claws, otherwise it may damage the furniture.
Training	Training requires patience. Most cats can be easily trained to use a litter box. A cat can learn to respond to its name (although it may not always come when you call it). Some cats can be trained to walk on a leash. Some can even learn to do tricks, such as shaking hands (paws) and retrieving a toy. Treats are helpful in teaching tricks.
Special notes	Since Bengals are energetic with a muscular build, it is important that they get plenty of exercise. Indoor "trees" or other cat-friendly objects can be used for climbing. This active breed needs enough food to fuel its high energy level.

BENGAL

IMAGINE A PET THAT LOOKS like an exotic wildcat but, at the same time, has all the affectionate, sweet-natured qualities of a domestic cat. The Bengal cat is one of the first cat breeds to be created by purposely crossing a domestic cat with a wildcat. It looks a lot like a small leopard, but it is completely tame. Owners say that Bengals make great pets and are just as loyal and loving as any domestic cat.

ORIGIN OF THE BENGAL

The Bengal is a fairly new cat breed, first developed by Jean Sugden, an American biologist, who cross-bred domestic cats and Asian leopard cats. The leopard cat is a small wildcat native to much of southern Asia. Matings with house cats occurred many times in the past, but none of the hybrids (crossbreeds) were kept.

DID YOU KNOW?
The Bengal cat's name comes from *Felis bengalensis*, the scientific name for the leopard cat.

Around 1960, Mrs. Sugden bred a pet female leopard cat with a black short-haired domestic male cat. The two cats produced a hybrid female kitten, which Mrs. Sugden named Kinkin. When Kinkin was older, she mated with her father and produced two kittens. One kitten was all black, but it had the temperament of a wild leopard cat and wouldn't let anyone go near it. The other kitten, a spotted male, had the sweet-natured temperament of a domestic cat.

This could have been the start of an exciting new breed of cat. However, Mrs. Sugden abandoned the project after her husband died, and the hybrid line died out. Years later, in the late 1970s, Mrs. Sugden (now Jean Mills after her remarriage) obtained eight female leopard cats–domestic hybrids from Dr. Willard Centerwall, a veterinary researcher at the University of California. Dr. Centerwall wanted to see if he could pass the leopard cat's natural immunity to feline leukemia on to its domestic offspring. Although that project did not work out, Mrs. Mills bred her hybrids to two male domestic cats, a red male and a brown spotted tabby. She was hoping to help stop the trade in exotic leopard cats by producing a domestic cat with the same looks. (Orphaned kittens of wild leopard cats were sold in pet shops at the time but generally wound up in zoos when they grew too wild for their owners to handle.)

Cats and Their Wild Ways

Although cats have been domesticated for thousands of years, they have kept many of their wild ways. A house cat may have no need to hunt down its prey while its owner supplies it with plenty of food, but a cat's hunting instincts make it hard for it to resist chasing after a mouse or trying to swat an insect flying around the house. The house cat may also practice its hunting skills by playing with small objects, tossing them into the air, and carrying them around.

A cat's senses are also good for hunting. Cats' eyes are good at picking up motion. They can quickly spot a scurrying mouse, a leaping grasshopper, or something else a cat might find interesting. You may have heard that cats can see in the dark. That's not exactly true: Cats can't see in complete darkness, but a reflecting layer at the back of the eyes lets them see fairly well in dim light—a useful ability for a night hunter.

When a mouse scurries across the floor, a cat feels the vibrations through the soles of its feet. The pads on a cat's paws and the hairs between them are very sensitive to touch. A cat can also use its whiskers (long, stiff hairs called vibrissae *on the upper lip, the chin, the cheeks, and above the eyes) to "feel" its way around a dark room and avoid bumping into things.*

In the first crosses, the male cats were not able to breed, but the females were. These hybrid cats, though, were often very nervous and skittish, like their wild ancestors. After a few generations of breeding with domestic males, the offspring had the looks of the leopard cats but the calmer disposition of domestic cats. Both males and females were fertile.

By 1983, the Bengal cat was recognized as a new breed by The International Cat Association, and in 1985, Bengal cats were exhibited in their first cat show. By 1989, there were an estimated 200 Bengal cats. Since then, they have become increasingly popular, and today there are at least 9,000 Bengals registered with cat clubs all over the world.

BENGALS AS PETS

The Bengal cat is a muscular, shorthaired breed. Its coat is soft and sleek and comes in two types of patterns: spotted (or "leopard") and marbled. Spotted Bengals have dark spots against a lighter background color. The spots may be solid black, dark brown, or rosetted (varying light/dark shades) on a light orange-tan or cream-colored background. Just as there are white tigers, there are also white Bengals, often called snow Bengals. The spots usually run horizontally on the Bengal's body, although they sometimes appear randomly. (Tabbies and other domestic cat breeds have vertical stripes or spots.) The marbled pattern, with dark whorls, comes from domestic tabby ancestors but runs horizontally.

Bengals are very active and intelligent animals. They are curious about their surroundings and are likely to get into things. They love to climb and may check out things from the top of a bookcase or mantel. So put away any breakable objects if you get a Bengal cat.

Bengals that are raised with plenty of love and attention enjoy being around people. Don't be surprised if your Bengal pet makes an unexpected visit while you are taking a bath or shower. Unlike most other domestic cats, Bengals *love* water. Bengal kittens are known for playing in their water bowls, and their toys are often found floating in their dishes.

Breeders say that before you buy a Bengal, make sure that it is at least four generations away from its wild ancestors. That way, your Bengal pet is more likely to be calm, with a sweet and affectionate personality.

INTERNET RESOURCES

www.gogees.com/ "Gogees—Perfecting the Bengal Breed"

www.defiant.net/info1.html "Bengal Cat FAQ"

www.thecatsite.com/breeds/bengal.html "The Bengal Cat"

www.i-love-cats.com/Breeds/bengal.htm "Cat Breed Descriptions: Bengal"

www.bengalcat.co.uk/pet/types/ "Bengal colours & patterns"

MAINE COON

FAST FACTS

Scientific name	*Felis catus* in Family Felidae, Order Carnivora
Cost	About $400 to $550 (more for show quality)
Food	Commercial cat food, water
Housing	Can be kept indoors or outdoors. Indoors, the cat may use a cat bed but will sleep anywhere it pleases. Provide cat toys to keep it busy and entertained; also a scratching post for sharpening its claws, otherwise it may damage the furniture.
Training	Training requires patience. Most cats can be easily trained to use a litter box. A cat can learn to respond to its name (although it may not always come when you call it). Some cats can be trained to walk on a leash. Some can even learn to do tricks, such as shaking hands (paws) and retrieving a toy. Treats are helpful in teaching tricks.
Special notes	Like any longhaired breed, the Maine coon cat needs regular grooming to maintain its smooth coat and keep it from becoming matted.

MAINE COON

OFTEN CALLED THE GENTLE GIANT of domestic cats, the Maine coon cat is one of the largest cat breeds and is known for its love for and devotion to its owners. Maine coons have been around since colonial times and are believed to be the first cats brought to the United States. These early cats got their name because they were thought to have originated in the state of Maine, and their bushy ringed tail looked a lot like that of a raccoon's.

ORIGIN OF THE MAINE COON CAT

No one knows for sure exactly where the Maine coon cat came from or how and when it came to the U.S. One folktale says that the Maine coon is the result of a crossing between semiwild domestic cats and raccoons. Of course this is biologically impossible, since these animals belong to two completely different species. Another theory is that the Maine coon was produced when domestic cats mated with bobcats. This would explain the Maine coon's tufts of hair sticking out of its ears and toes and the cat's large size. But this is also rather unlikely.

Before Columbus?

Several theories link the Maine coon's origin to Norwegian forest cats, which look very similar. Some of these cats may have been brought to North America by Viking explorers, 500 years before Christopher Columbus. Old Viking maps show that they were familiar with this continent, and some of their ships' cats could have come ashore to make a home in the New World. (Cats were often taken aboard ships because they were very helpful in controlling the rat population, as well as keeping the sailors company.)

One of the most romantic stories about the Maine coon cat ties its origin to Marie Antoinette, the Queen of France. Supposedly, when Marie Antoinette was trying to escape France during the French Revolution, she sent her most prized possessions—furniture, china, silver, ornaments, and her six longhaired Angora cats—aboard a ship called the *Sally*. Unfortunately, Marie Antoinette was unable to follow because she was beheaded before she had a chance to get out of France. The captain of the *Sally*, Samuel Clough, brought the queen's cats and the rest of her belongings to Wincasset, Maine. Once there, the Angora cats are said to have mated with the local short-haired cats to eventually produce the Maine coon breed.

We may never be able to uncover the mysteries of the Maine coon's true origin. What we do know is that the Maine coon breed is the result of surviving Maine's cold, harsh climate. Through natural selection, only the strongest cats survived. They developed into large, rugged cats with long, thick, water-resistant coats, protecting them from the bitter-cold winters.

Maine coons started to become popular in the early 1860s, when New England farmers, recognizing the beauty of these cats, held an annual cat show at the Skowhegan Fair. Maine coons from all over the area were competing for the title of "Maine State Champion Coon Cat."

Maine coon cats became extremely popular and did quite well in the first official cat shows. However, their popularity did not last. By the early 1900s, Persians, Angoras, and other exotic cats were fast becoming the new favorites. By the 1940s, Maine coons were seldom seen on the cat show circuit. In 1953 a small group of breeders formed the Central Maine Coon Cat Club to keep this breed from disappearing forever. The club held cat shows for Maine coon cats only, just like those back in the 1860s. In 1968 the Maine Coon Breeders and Fanciers Association was founded. Soon Maine coons were competing for championships in general cat shows again. Today, the Maine coon cat is among the most popular longhaired cats.

> **DID YOU KNOW?**
> The Maine coon cat was actually the first cat breed to be exhibited at American cat shows. It wasn't until 1895 that the first official cat show took place in North America (in New York)—more than thirty years after the Maine coon started participating in competitive cat shows.

MAINE COONS AS PETS

The Maine coon cat is a large, sturdy breed. Males generally weigh 12 to 18 pounds (5.4 to 8 kilograms), although some may be more than 20 pounds (9 kilograms). Females are usually smaller, ranging from 8 to 12 pounds (3.6 to 5.4 kilograms), although some may be as much as 14 pounds (6.4 kilograms). The Maine coon's long, shaggy hair often makes the cat look bigger than it actually is.

Maine coons can come in a wide variety of colors, although brown tabby is the most common color and pattern. Its long, thick coat is smooth and silky and doesn't get knotted up as easily as the coats of some other longhaired breeds. However, as with any longhaired cat, regular grooming is very important in keeping the coat tangle-free. A Maine coon's long, bushy tail is one of its most recognizable traits. The early Maine coons had a more distinctly ringed tail than those of today.

Maine coons make affectionate and lovable pets. These gentle giants love to be around people and will follow their owners around the house. They are very curious creatures and will investigate any drawer or cabinet left open. Maine coons are not very vocal, but will make chirping sounds to communicate with their owners. They are also known for standing on their hind legs to check out their surroundings. This behavior is unusual for large breeds but is more typical of smaller, slender cats.

Maine coons are also fascinated by water. Don't be surprised if you catch your pet playing in the water dish or licking from the water faucet. Getting wet does not bother these cats as much as other breeds, perhaps because of their thick, waterproof coat.

INTERNET RESOURCES

www.cfainc.org/breeds/profiles/maine.html "CFA Breed Profile: Maine Coon"

www.cfainc.org/breeds/profiles/articles/maine.html "Breed Article: America's First Show Cat—The Maine Coon Cat"

www.fanciers.com/breed-faqs/maine-coon-faq.html "The Maine Coon: Cat Breed FAQ"

www.nwlink.com/~conniez/introduc.htm "Introducing the Maine Coon Cat"

www.i-love-cats.com/Breeds/mainecoon.htm "Cat Breed Descriptions: Maine Coon"

MANX

FAST FACTS

Scientific name	*Felis catus* in Family Felidae, Order Carnivora
Cost	About $150 to $300 (more for show quality)
Food	Commercial cat food, water
Housing	Can be kept indoors or outdoors. Indoors, the cat may use a cat bed but will sleep anywhere it pleases. Provide cat toys to keep it busy and entertained; also a scratching post for sharpening its claws, otherwise it may damage the furniture.
Training	Training requires patience. Most cats can be easily trained to use a litter box. A cat can learn to respond to its name (although it may not always come when you call it). Some cats can be trained to walk on a leash. Some can even learn to do tricks, such as shaking hands (paws) and retrieving a toy. Treats are helpful in teaching tricks.
Special notes	Some experts say that the Manx's back is weak, which could make walking difficult. Therefore, this area should be strengthened through exercise, which should involve forms of play such as leaping and climbing.

MANX

CAN YOU IMAGINE A CAT without a tail? Cats are famous for their long, sweeping tails, but Manx cats are often born without a tail or with just a short stump of a tail. This cat looks like it's missing something. But Manx owners love its adorable face and sweet-natured personality.

While a "tailless" cat may make for interesting conversation, this pet may not be right for everyone. This breed is more likely to have health problems than other domestic cats. A Manx may require more care than the average cat, and owners should know what to look for in case any problems do develop.

Cat Tails

A cat's tail is actually a part of its spine (backbone), which is made up of tiny, individual bones, called vertebrae, *linked together. This arrangement makes the spine very flexible, able to twist and turn. Cats use their tails to help keep their balance. For example, when a cat falls, it whips its tail around and twists its body to turn over and land on its feet. The tail also helps a cat walk across a narrow ledge or tree branch. Lacking a tail, Manx cats may have trouble keeping their balance.*

Cats also use their tails to express their feelings. A happy, satisfied cat will hold its tail up high. A sad or nervous cat will hold its tail down low. Swishing the tail rapidly back and forth means the cat is annoyed. A Manx cannot show its emotions in these ways.

THE MANX GENE

Why are Manx often born without a typical cat tail? Hundreds of years ago a mutation, or change, occurred in the genes of the Manx cat population. (Genes are complicated chemicals that determine inherited traits, such as fur color and body size.) Breeders call this mutation the *Manx gene*, and it can make breeding Manx cats pretty tricky. Litters are often small, with an average of two to three kittens. Manx kittens have a higher death rate than any other domestic cat.

When a tailless cat mates with another cat, the kittens are likely to be born with a shortened tail or no tail at all, even if just one of the parents has the Manx gene. If both parents have the Manx gene, the kittens are likely to die before birth. Those that do survive may develop serious health problems. The Manx gene causes changes in the formation of the entire spine, not just the tail. The cat may develop back problems or be born with a serious condition called *spina bifida*. However, breeders say health problems can be avoided through careful breeding.

There are actually four types of Manx cats. *Rumpies* are completely tailless; there is just a dimple at the end where a tail would normally be. This is the only kind allowed to be shown at cat shows. The *rumpy riser* has a little rise of bone at the end of the spine instead of a dimple. The *stumpy* has a very short tail that looks like a stub. The *longie* does have a tail, which may be quite long. Breeders usually mate a rumpy with a partially tailed Manx to get tailless kittens.

A Manx Look-alike

The Japanese bobtail is sometimes mistaken for a Manx. These two breeds are not related, and their shortened tails are due to different genetic mutations. Both parents must have a Japanese bobtail gene to produce a litter of bobtails, whereas a tailless or stub-tailed Manx is produced when only one parent carries the Manx gene. Also, the Japanese bobtail gene is not linked to any health problems involving the spine or bones.

The Japanese bobtail has a very short tail; it is never tailless like the typical show Manx. The bobtail's tail may be stubby, curved, or kinked and looks like a pom-pom. This breed has been admired in Japan for hundreds of years, where it is considered a symbol of good luck. It is now becoming popular in the United States.

ORIGIN OF THE MANX CAT

The Manx is one of the oldest cat breeds. It is believed to have developed hundreds of years ago on the Isle of Man, an island in the Irish Sea between England and Ireland. Cats with tails were most likely brought over by visiting ships. Isolated on this island, the small group of cats bred with one another. The rare Manx gene became more common among them as it was passed from one generation to the next. Eventually, these cats established their own distinct tailless breed.

The natives of Isle of Man made up a number of tall tales to explain the tailless cats. Some said the Manx is the result of a cross between a cat and a rabbit. Others suggested that two Manx cats lost their tails when a door slammed on them as they were boarding Noah's Ark!

Manx cats were first exhibited in cat shows in Britain in the late nineteenth century. They reached North American cat shows in 1899. The Manx was recognized as a cat breed in the 1920s. Today, there is a huge demand for Manx cats, but there are not enough available due to the breeding difficulties.

MANX AS PETS

The Manx is a medium-sized cat with a compact, muscular body and a round face. Males weigh an average 8 to 12 pounds (3.6 to 5.4 kilograms), females between 6 and 10 pounds (2.7 to 4.5 kilograms). Manx come in a wide variety of colors and patterns. Their coat is thick and may be either shorthaired or longhaired. Of course they are most noted for being tailless, but remember there are Manx with a variety of tail lengths.

The Manx has a curved backside, due to the fact that its hind legs are longer than the front legs. In fact, the Manx walks or runs with a "bunny hop." The hind legs are very strong, and the Manx can jump, climb, run, and hunt very well.

Manx are sometimes called the "dog cat" because they tend to behave like dogs in some ways. They are very protective of their homes, and these "watch cats" may even let out a little growl if they are disturbed or hear a strange noise. They also follow their owners around the house and check out what they are doing. They like to retrieve, and sometimes bury their toys, much like what a dog would do.

Despite the risk of health problems, Manx are hardy cats. When cared for properly, they can live fifteen years or more.

INTERNET RESOURCES

www.cfainc.org/breeds/profiles/manx.html "CFA Breed Profile: Manx"

www.cfainc.org/breeds/profiles/articles/manx.html "Breed Article: Manx"

www.fanciers.com/breed-faqs/manx-faq.html "The Manx: Cat Breed FAQ"

www.i-love-cats.com/Breeds/manx.htm "Cat Breed Descriptions: Manx"

FAST FACTS

Scientific name	*Felis catus* in Family Felidae, Order Carnivora
Cost	Between $250 and $500
Food	Commercial cat food, water
Housing	Can be kept indoors or outdoors. However, the Persian is recommended as an indoor cat because it has a sedentary lifestyle, and its fur is more likely to get matted outdoors. Indoors, the cat may use a cat bed but will sleep anywhere it pleases. Provide cat toys to keep it busy and entertained; also a scratching post for sharpening its claws, otherwise it may damage the furniture.
Training	Training requires patience. Most cats can be easily trained to use a litter box. A cat can learn to respond to its name (although it may not always come when you call it). Some cats can be trained to walk on a leash. Some can even learn to do tricks, such as shaking hands (paws) and retrieving a toy. Treats are helpful in teaching tricks.
Special notes	Regular grooming is very important to keep the hair free from tangles. Also, tests show that close to 40 percent of Persians may develop PKD, a hereditary kidney disease.

PERSIAN

HOW MANY CAT BREEDS could you name before reading this book? If you're like most people, you had probably heard about maybe two or three cat breeds—and one of them was the Persian. Persian cats are probably the most popular of all cat breeds. They are famous for their long, silky hair and jewel-like eyes, which give them a look of beauty and elegance.

Persians are sweet-natured cats that provide their owners with plenty of love and affection. However, a Persian's long hair needs to be groomed regularly, or serious problems may develop. If you cannot keep up with its grooming needs, this longhaired breed may not be for you.

ORIGIN OF THE PERSIAN CAT

The Persian's exact origin is not known, but it is believed that this breed originally came from Asia, most likely Persia (now Iran) and Turkey. Persian soldiers who conquered Egypt in 525 B.C. may have taken Egyptian cats back home with them. Over the centuries, longhaired varieties appeared among the domestic cats of the Middle East. Angora cats, white cats with long, silky fur and a slender build, were bred in Turkey. (*Angora* comes from the name of the Turkish capital, Ankara.) Cats with long, thick fur and a stocky build became common in Persia. These traits are good for survival in extremely cold weather, and yet, it is quite hot in most of Persia. Cat historians are not sure whether the Persian type developed in the cold, rugged mountains of the Khorasan district in eastern Persia, or whether the thick fur and stocky build came from longhaired Russian cats that interbred with the local domestic cats.

> **DID YOU KNOW?**
> Persians are said to be one of the quietest and least active of all cat breeds. They are also more likely than other breeds to accept other cats into their home.

Ancestors of today's Persians, Angoras, and other longhaired cat breeds were first introduced into Europe by travelers from Persia in the late 1500s. It was reported that an Italian traveler, Pietro della Valle, brought some Persian cats into Italy during the early 1600s. Writing about his voyage, della Valle described the

Persians as "gray with very long, silky, glossy fur." Other travelers brought Persians and Angoras into France, and then into England, where they quickly became popular. For a long time, these cats were very rare and greatly prized.

For centuries, Persian cats were commonly crossbred with Turkish Angoras and other long-haired breeds. The fur of the original Persians was thicker and a little coarser than that of the Angoras. Some people say this cross may be responsible for the Persian's long, silky coat we know today. Persians were a hit at the first modern cat show, held at the Crystal Palace in London in 1871. The Persian was admired for its beauty and elegance, and breeders soon began working to improve the breed. By the early 1900s, the Persian cat was popular all over the world and often took top prize at cat shows. Its popularity continues to this day.

The Persian's Cousin

As Persian and Siamese cats became popular during the early 1900s, breeders longed to produce a longhaired cat with Siamese markings. The first efforts began during the 1920s, but the goal was not achieved until the 1930s. A long series of careful matings between Persians and Siamese produced a new kind of Persian, called the Himalayan. This is a longhaired cat, with the body build of a Persian and the markings of a Siamese. Once the breed was established, it was no longer necessary to use Siamese. The breeding program was continued using matings of Himalayans with Himalayans. After a number of generations of such breeding, however, the cats start to lose some of the Persian traits. So breeders today sometimes mate Himalayans back to Persians.

Himalayans may be a bit livelier than Persians, but they are far more easygoing than the Siamese ancestors who provided the color markings. They are very affectionate and attentive to humans. Their striking appearance and pleasing personality have made Himalayan cats very popular.

PERSIAN CATS AS PETS

The Persian is a medium- to large-sized cat with small ears and a stocky, muscular body. It is known for its long, silky, two-layered coat, which may have hairs up to 6 inches (15 centimeters) long. Today, Persian cats come in a wide variety of colors and patterns, including jet-black, pure white, blue, red, brown, gray, tabby-striped, and the tortoiseshell or calico pattern (tricolor). An especially beautiful variety is the chinchilla Persian, whose white hairs are tipped with black, giving the fur a silvery sheen.

These days, Persians are being developed with a flattened, pushed-in face, with the nose and mouth level with the eyes. This Persian variety is commonly seen in cat shows. The traditional doll-faced Persian, however, is more proportioned, with its nose and mouth sticking out in front of the eyes. Critics claim that the sunken look of the modern Persian may cause breathing problems. The cats' eyes may tend to water because the tears don't drain properly, and their teeth are crowded, which may result in dental problems.

Owners say that a Persian makes a wonderful pet because it is sweet-natured and affectionate. It is not a very active breed and doesn't mind just hanging out and watching the world go by. Of course it does have playful moments; but for the most part, a Persian cat would rather stay in one place than run around.

If a Persian's long, beautiful coat is not brushed regularly, it will mat up very easily. Eventually, the mats pull at the cat's skin and sores may develop. (Flies have even been known to lay eggs in a cat's sores!) Then the cat needs medical attention, and the fur has to be shaved off. So if you want a luxurious cat like the Persian, be prepared for lots of grooming.

INTERNET RESOURCES

www.cfainc.org/breeds/profiles/persian.html "CFA Breed Profile: Persian"

www.thecatsite.com/breeds/persian.html "The Persian Cat"

www.i-love-cats.com/Breeds/persian.html "Cat Breed Descriptions: Persian"

www.cfainc.org/breeds/profiles/persian-him.html "CFA Persian Breed Profile: Himalayan Division"

FAST FACTS

Scientific name	*Felis catus* in Family Felidae, Order Carnivora
Cost	Between $350 and $700
Food	Commercial cat food, water
Housing	Can be kept indoors or outdoors. (The ultra-shorthaired Cornish rex may prefer the indoors in a cold climate.) Indoors, the cat may use a cat bed but will sleep anywhere it pleases. Provide cat toys to keep it busy and entertained; also a scratching post for sharpening its claws, otherwise it may damage the furniture.
Training	Training requires patience. Most cats can be easily trained to use a litter box. A cat can learn to respond to its name (although it may not always come when you call it). Some cats can be trained to walk on a leash. Some can even learn to do tricks, such as shaking hands (paws) and retrieving a toy. Treats are helpful in teaching tricks.
Special notes	Very little grooming is needed for the Cornish rex breed. They have wash-and-go hair, and when bathed, it dries almost immediately. This breed needs enough food to support its active lifestyle.

REX

HAVE YOU EVER SEEN a rex cat? It looks like it got a perm at a beauty salon. Its body is covered with wavy, kinky-looking fur. These wavy curls aren't made by curlers or a curling iron—they are natural, and they are characteristic of the rex breeds.

Some people say that rex cats look like they are from outer space, not just because of their unusual coat but also because of their big bright eyes and enormous batlike ears. But owners say it doesn't take long to become attached to these fun-loving and affectionate cats.

THE ORIGIN OF REX CATS

In July 1950, on a farm in Cornwall, England, a cat named Serena gave birth to a male kitten with an unusual curly coat. His four brothers and sisters all had straight coats. The cats' owner, Nina Ennismore, tried to smooth out the curls by drying the kitten's coat, only to find that it became even curlier. She decided to keep the curly-coated kitten and named him Kallibunker. Mrs. Ennismore knew that the curly trait was the result of a gene mutation because she used to breed rex rabbits, whose coats are also wavy. On the advice of a genetics expert, she crossed Kallibunker back to his mother so that the curly gene could be passed on. Serena soon gave birth to a litter of three kittens: a female with a straight coat and two curly-coated males. This was the start of a new cat breed, which Mrs. Ennismore called the Cornish rex, after the breed's place of origin (Cornwall) and the curly-coated rex rabbit.

In 1957, two Cornish rexes came to the United States. One of them died shortly after it arrived. The other, named LaMorna Cove, was pregnant by one of Serena's sons, Poldhu, and produced a litter of two rex kittens, Diamond Lil and Marmaduke. These cats are the ancestors of the Cornish rex cats in the United States.

When closely related animals breed together, health problems may develop after a few genera-

> **DID YOU KNOW?**
> A rex cat's fur is not the only thing that's curly; its whiskers are, too!

tions. That is because the offspring may get two of any "bad genes"—one from each parent. So the American breeders were not surprised when they mated Diamond Lil with her brother, Marmaduke, and all of the kittens in the litter died. To keep the rex line going, they bred Diamond Lil and Marmaduke to Siamese cats. The litters were all straight-haired, but some of *their* offspring were curly-coated rexes. (The curly-coat trait in rex cats appears only if a kitten inherits the gene from both parents.) Rex cats were also bred to other shorthair breeds. These "outcrosses" produced healthy kittens and also provided the varied coat colors of today's Cornish rex cats. Now that there are enough Cornish rex cats, outcrossing is no longer necessary.

What's Under That Coat?

The curly coat of a Cornish rex cat is different from that of any other shorthaired cat. Most cats have a coat made up of three types of hairs: guard hairs, awn hairs, and down hairs. The top layers (guard and awn hairs) are much longer and coarser than down hairs. The down hairs, which are very soft, make up the undercoat. The Cornish rex cat does not have any guard or awn hairs—only down hairs. The down coat is not woolly like a lamb's or coarse like a poodle's. It is as soft as silk, softer than any other cat's coat, yet feels plush like velvet.

In 1960, a woman named Beryl Cox from Devon, England, noticed a curly-coated tomcat hanging around her neighborhood. The tomcat mated with a straight-coated female, who produced a litter that included a kitten with a curly coat, just like his father's. Ms. Cox named this curly-coated kitten Kirlee. She had seen pictures of the Cornish rex and thought that Kirlee might be one, too. So she called Brian Stirling-Webb, a Cornish rex breeder, and they decided to breed Kirlee with Cornish rex cats. To their surprise, matings between Kirlee and Cornish rex females produced only straight-coated kittens. It was clear that Kirlee was not a Cornish rex, and also that a different curly gene was involved. A new breeding program began, and Kirlee was the founding father of a new rex breed, the Devon rex.

By 1967, Great Britain recognized the Devon rex as a separate breed from the Cornish rex. That meant that they could now compete in cat shows under two separate breed standards. In North America, however, both Cornish and Devon rexes were generally shown in the same category under the rex name. Devon rex breeders were unhappy about this because their cats were judged by the Cornish rex standards. This finally changed in 1979 when the Cornish rex and Devon rex were recognized as two separate breeds. Through the years, a number of other rex cat breeds have been discovered.

REX CATS AS PETS

The Cornish rex cat is the most popular type of rex to keep as a pet, with the Devon rex a close second. Rex cats are small to medium-sized animals, weighing between 4 and 9 pounds (1.8 to 4 kilograms). They are slender, yet muscular, and have a triangle-shaped face with large satellite-dish ears. The Cornish rex is an ultra short-haired cat that has just the undercoat, but the Devon rex has both awn hairs and down hairs. Other rex breeds, such as the Selkirk and LaPerm, are longhaired. All rex breeds, however, have some type of curvy, wavy, or ripply coat.

> **DID YOU KNOW?**
> Rex cats have very good appetites. Don't forget to feed them, or they will let you know. Normally these cats are not very vocal, but they are when it comes to their food.

Rex cats are very active animals. They don't mind sitting on a lap once in a while, but they prefer to run around and play. Owning a rex is like owning a lifelong kitten. These cats are very intelligent and very curious. They will follow you around the house to check out your every move. They can also learn to get into cabinets and drawers. They can pick up objects with their paws and carry things around in their mouth. They like to check out their surroundings from high places, such as a tall bookshelf or a refrigerator.

Owners say that rex cats make wonderful pets because they are sweet, affectionate, and highly entertaining to watch. But these cats are very social animals and will not be happy if they are left alone for long periods of time. If they don't get enough attention from their owners, it would probably be a good idea to get another cat to keep the rex company.

INTERNET RESOURCES

www.cfainc.org/breeds/profiles/cornish.html "CFA Breed Profile: Cornish Rex"

www.cfainc.org/breeds/profiles/devon.html "CFA Breed Profile: Devon Rex"

www.i-love-cats.com/Breeds/cornishrex.htm "Cat Breed Descriptions: Cornish Rex"

www.i-love-cats.com/Breeds/devonrex.htm "Cat Breed Descriptions: Devon Rex"

www.catsinfo.com/cornishrex.html "Cornish Rex"

www.catsinfo.com/devonrex.html "Devon Rex"

www.geocities.com/Broadway/1222/crex_faq.html "Cornish Rex FAQ"

www.catsandkittens.com/breeds/crex.shtml "Cornish Rex: Totally Eclipsing"

www.descornex.com/Characteristics.htm "Characteristics of the Cornish Rex Cat"

FAST FACTS

Scientific name	*Felis catus* in Family Felidae, Order Carnivora
Cost	About $300 to $400 for pet quality (up to $800 for show quality)
Food	Commercial cat food, water
Housing	Can be kept indoors or outdoors. Indoors, the cat may use a cat bed but will sleep anywhere it pleases. Provide cat toys to keep it busy and entertained; also a scratching post for sharpening its claws, otherwise it may damage the furniture.
Training	Training requires patience. Most cats can be easily trained to use a litter box. A cat can learn to respond to its name (although it may not always come when you call it). Some cats can be trained to walk on a leash. Some can even learn to do tricks, such as shaking hands (paws) and retrieving a toy. Treats are helpful in teaching tricks.
Special notes	This breed is not a good choice of pet for someone who is away at work or school most of the day, unless it has another cat to keep it company.

SCOTTISH FOLD

IT'S HARD TO IMAGINE a cat without those triangle-shaped ears. But the Scottish fold cat almost looks like it doesn't have any ears. Its ears are bent down against its head, instead of pointing straight up like those of most cats. A Scottish fold cat, with its folded ears, sweet, round face, and large bright eyes, looks a bit like a little furry owl.

What Makes a Cat's Ears Fold?

All kittens, whether they are fold-eared or not, appear normal when they are born. At this time, their ears are made of soft, rubbery cartilage. (It is cartilage that allows our ears to bend.) After about fifteen to twenty-five days, the ears start to harden, causing them to stand upright. But Scottish folds' ears start to bend forward, giving them their characteristic folded ears.

ORIGIN OF THE SCOTTISH FOLD CAT

The first Scottish fold cat was a white barn cat, named Susie, discovered in 1961 on a farm near Coupar Angus in Scotland. A shepherd, William Ross, first noticed Susie at his neighbor's barn. Mr. Ross was very curious about this cat's strange, folded ears. He thought they looked a lot like those of lop rabbits, which also have folded ears. When he got home, William told his wife, Mary, about the fold-eared cat.

A few days later, the Rosses went next door and asked their neighbors, the McRaes, about Susie's origins. The McRaes did not know much about Susie's background but promised that if Susie ever had a litter of fold-eared kittens, they would give one to the Rosses. A year later, Susie gave birth to two fold-eared kittens, one male and one female. The McRaes gave the male to another neighbor, who had it neutered and kept it as a pet. The female was given to William and Mary Ross, who named her Snooks. Snooks was a beautiful, white fold-eared cat, just like her mother. Sadly, a few months later, Susie was hit by a car and killed.

The Rosses, who already owned a Siamese cat, thought that Snooks could be the start of developing a brand-new breed. At this point, they called the breed the lop-eared cat. Snooks gave birth to a number of fold-eared kittens. The Rosses went to cat shows to see if people would be interested in this new breed. They were told to contact Pat Turner, a breeder who was interested in cat genetics. Pat visited the Rosses and took Snowdrift, a white fold-eared male, back home with her to start a scientific breeding program.

Soon Pat Turner bred Snowdrift to her own show cat, a white British shorthair. Over the next three years, Ms. Turner crossed British shorthairs with the fold-eared and straight-eared offspring of Snowdrift. During this time, the experimental breeding program produced seventy-six kittens—forty-two with folded ears and thirty-four with straight ears. She and a fellow genetics expert, Peter Dyte, concluded that the fold ears can appear even if just one parent had the fold gene.

Soon the breed's name was changed from lop-eared to folds after Pat Turner explained to the Rosses that the ear fold of rabbits is not really the same as the cats', and therefore, the name is not accurate. In lop-eared rabbits, the fold occurs at the base of the ear, whereas the fold in cats occurs higher on the ear.

The Scottish fold was not accepted by the British Cat Fancy and was banned from cat shows in Great Britain. This decision was based on the idea that Scottish Folds were more likely to experience deafness or develop ear diseases than other breeds. Actually, this is not true. There is no evidence that this breed has a higher risk of health problems than any other breed.

The Rosses realized that the only way for the Scottish fold to be accepted would be to take it to another country. In 1970, three Scottish folds were sent to the United States, where they were received by Neil Todd, a genetics expert in Massachusetts. On November 30, 1971, two Scottish fold kittens, a male named Romeo and a female named Juliet, were born. After a few years, Dr. Todd lost interest in breeding Scottish folds and found homes for the cats bred at his research center. One of these cats went to Salle Wolfe Peters, a Manx breeder in Pennsylvania, who decided to start her own Scottish fold breeding program. Mrs. Peters is mainly responsible for developing the Scottish fold breed in the United States.

In 1973, the first Scottish fold cat was registered in the United States. By 1978, the breed achieved championship standing at cat shows. Today, the Scottish fold cat is among the top ten most popular cat breeds in U.S. cat shows.

SCOTTISH FOLDS AS PETS

The Scottish fold is a medium-sized cat, males weighing an average 9 to 13 pounds (4 to 6 kilograms) and females about 6 to 9 pounds (2.7 to 4 kilograms). This cat's small ears are folded downward and forward, making its head look rounded. The way the ears are folded varies. Some have a single fold, others a double or even a triple fold. The Scottish fold's large, round eyes and subtle "smile" give these cats a sweet-looking expression. There are shorthaired and longhaired varieties of this breed, although shorthaired folds seem to be more popular.

Scottish folds are smart, sweet-natured cats. They are not a very active breed, and are known for being rather easygoing and laid-back. They can adapt well to new people and new situations. They are very affectionate and usually form a bond with one particular person in the household, although they won't refuse anyone who wants to pet or cuddle them.

Scottish folds have very soft voices, which sound more like squeaks than meows. Sometimes they even let out a "silent meow." That's when they open their mouth to speak, but no sound comes out.

DID YOU KNOW?
Cats with single folds are usually kept as pets. Show cats usually have a double or triple fold.

Scottish folds are very curious and will follow you around the house to see what you are doing. These cats love company and do not like being left alone too long. So if you can't spend enough time with your Scottish fold pet, it is probably a good idea to get another cat companion.

INTERNET RESOURCES

www.cfainc.org/breeds/profiles/scottish.html "CFA Breed Profile: Scottish Fold"

www.fanciers.com/breed-faqs/scottish-fold-faq.html "Scottish Fold: Cat Breed FAQ"

www.i-love-cats.com/Breeds/scottishfold.htm "Cat Breed Descriptions: Scottish Fold"

www.petsmart.com/aspca/cats/scottish_fold.shtml "ASPCA Complete Guide to Cats: Scottish Fold"

www.homepet.com/scottish/scott-an.htm "The Scottish Fold Cat"

www.catsandkittens.com/breeds/scotfold.shtml "The Scottish Fold"

FAST FACTS

Scientific name	*Felis catus* in Family Felidae, Order Carnivora
Cost	About $200 to $500
Food	Commercial cat food, water
Housing	Can be kept indoors or outdoors. Indoors, the cat may use a cat bed but will sleep anywhere it pleases. Provide cat toys to keep it busy and entertained; also a scratching post for sharpening its claws, otherwise it may damage the furniture.
Training	Training requires patience. Most cats can be easily trained to use a litter box. A cat can learn to respond to its name (although it may not always come when you call it). Some cats can be trained to walk on a leash. Some can even learn to do tricks, such as shaking hands (paws) and retrieving a toy. Treats are helpful in teaching tricks.
Special notes	This active breed needs plenty of exercise. You can buy indoor "trees" or other cat-friendly objects for climbing. Diet is also very important. A Siamese cat needs enough food to fuel its high energy level. Also, provide this cat with plenty of toys to play with to avoid boredom, or it will find its own way to pass the time.

SIAMESE

SIAMESE

THE SIAMESE CAT IS probably the most easily recognized of all cat breeds. Its long, sleek body, triangular face, and bright blue eyes give the Siamese a very elegant, striking appearance. And of course, its unusual coat pattern is what makes this cat look unique. The Siamese coat has a darker coloring on its "points"—face, ears, feet, and tail—and a much lighter coloring on its neck and body.

Temperature Tells the Tale

All Siamese kittens are born entirely white. They do not develop their dark-colored points until weeks after birth. That's because the color change in Siamese kittens depends on their body temperature. Siamese cats carry special white-fur genes that work only when the body temperature is above 98°F (36.7°C). Normally a cat's body temperature is about 100°F (37.8°C). But it tends to lose heat more quickly from its head, slender limbs, and tail. The temperature of these "points" drops to about 96°F (35.6°C), and the dark coloring is produced. If the kittens are kept in a very warm room, their points will not darken, and they will remain a creamy white. (Siamese kittens are born white because they were warm and cozy in their mother's body.) As the kittens grow older and more independent, their points become cooler and gradually darken.

ORIGIN OF THE SIAMESE CAT

The Siamese cat is one of the oldest cat breeds. It is believed to have originated in Siam (now Thailand). The earliest records of the breed appear in *The Cat-Book Poems*, written sometime between 1350 and 1767 (most likely around the 1500s) in the ancient Siamese capital of Ayudhya. This book included drawings of various kinds of cats, one of which depicted what we now know as the Siamese cat. It was later given the name Siamese because it was the first cat from Siam seen in the Western world, and the most unusual-looking one.

The Siamese breed has been called "the royal cat of Siam." Only the royal family and wealthy nobles were allowed to own Siamese cats. Cats owned by the

King of Siam were said to be trained to guard his palace walls, warning him of intruders with their loud cries. They were also given as gifts to visiting nobles and high officials by the royalty of Siam.

No one is sure exactly when Siamese cats first came to England. Records show that in 1884 the King of Siam gave a pair of seal point Siamese cats to Owen Gould, the British consul-general in Bangkok, who sent them to his sister in England. These cats created quite a stir when they were exhibited at a cat show the following year at the Crystal Palace in London. However, Siamese cats had been described back in 1871 as an "unnatural nightmare kind of cat." Despite these unkind words, the breed sparked a lot of interest among cat lovers. A small group of less than a dozen Siamese cats imported into Britain in the 1800s provided the basis for today's popular Siamese breed.

In 1890, the first Siamese cats were introduced to the United States; they were a gift from the King of Siam to an American friend. Some other Siamese were imported from England to the U.S. At first they were strictly cats for rich people. It cost about a thousand dollars to bring a cat over from England—quite a lot of money at the turn of the century. Since the beginning, Siamese cats have been one of the most popular breeds at cat shows in both England and the United States.

SIAMESE CATS AS PETS

There are two body types for a Siamese cat: the traditional type and the modern, or extreme, type. The traditional Siamese cat is much larger and stockier than the modern type, with a rounder, apple-shaped head. The modern Siamese cat is very slender, with skinny legs and a triangle-shaped head. Modern Siamese are the ones most likely to be show cats.

There is a controversy between breeders of the two body types. Those who fancy the traditional Siamese would like to preserve the breed because they believe that their rounder, stockier build looks more like the original Siamese, before humans started to develop it into today's slender appearance. On the other hand, breeders of the modern Siamese believe that their sleek Siamese breed is actually more like the original type of Siamese. So who is correct? No one can say for sure. Whether they are slender or stocky, though, all Siamese cats still have the striking blue eyes of their ancestors.

Siamese cats are a shorthaired breed. There are four classic coat types: seal (dark brown) point, chocolate point, blue point, and lilac point. Remember, *point* refers to the color on the face, ears, feet, and tail. Newer color points were later developed, including red, cream, tabby, and tortoiseshell.

Siamese cats are among the most active of all cat breeds. They love to play and investigate. This cat doesn't like to be left alone, and, if bored, could find its way into trouble. Siamese cats have gotten a bad reputation for being nasty or vicious. Many owners of Siamese cats would say that this is not true. Like any cat, a Siamese needs plenty of love and affection to build a close bond with its owner. Sometimes it may want to snuggle up in your lap, and other times it may want its space. Siamese cats are typically quite bossy and tend to dominate other cats in the household.

Siamese cats are known for having a very loud, hoarse voice. They are much more "talkative" than other breeds. If a Siamese cat wants something—whether it wants to eat, go outside, or play—it usually lets you know about it. It can be quite demanding and is not likely to stop "talking" until it gets what it wants. Sometimes it seems like the cat just wants to talk a lot about nothing. Some people may find their highly talkative nature rather annoying, while others find it charming.

> **DID YOU KNOW?**
> The Siamese cat is considered a "natural" breed. That means that the ancestors of a registered cat must all have been of the same cat breed. However, Siamese cats have been used to develop many of today's other cat breeds, including the Himalayan, Burmese, Tonkinese, Snowshoe, and various Oriental breeds.

INTERNET RESOURCES

www.cfainc.org/breeds/profiles/siamese.html "CFA Breed Profile: Siamese"

www.i-love-cats.com/Breeds/siamese.htm "Cat Breed Descriptions: Siamese"

nd.essortment.com/siamesecatpet_ozx.htm "Information on Siamese cats"

www.petsmart.com/aspca/cats/siamese.html "Siamese"

FAST FACTS

Scientific name	*Felis catus* in Family Felidae, Order Carnivora
Cost	About $800 to $1200
Food	Commercial cat food, water
Housing	Should be kept indoors, since its lack of coat makes it vulnerable to cold and hot temperatures. The cat may use a cat bed but will sleep anywhere it pleases. Provide cat toys to keep it busy and entertained; also a scratching post for sharpening its claws, otherwise it may damage the furniture.
Training	Training requires patience. Most cats can be easily trained to use a litter box. A cat can learn to respond to its name (although it may not always come when you call it). Some cats can be trained to walk on a leash. Some can even learn to do tricks, such as shaking hands (paws) and retrieving a toy. Treats are helpful in teaching tricks.
Special notes	The sphynx must be bathed regularly to remove excess oils in the skin. This cat needs large amounts of food to support its high energy level and maintain its body heat. Food should be available throughout the day.

SPHYNX

COMMONLY CALLED THE "hairless cat," the sphynx is probably the most unusual of all cat breeds. But this cat isn't really hairless. The sphynx's body is actually covered with very short, thin down hairs, especially on the cat's ears, nose, tail, and paws. Its body is smooth and silky, and stroking it feels like touching suede. Big lemon-shaped eyes and large batlike ears add to the sphynx's oddball looks. Combine that with a playful and affectionate personality, and owning a sphynx is a unique experience.

Allergy-Free Cats?

You might think that a hairless cat is the perfect solution for someone who is allergic to cats. Actually, however, there is no such thing as an allergy-free cat, even if it doesn't have fluffy cat hair. It is not a cat's hair that makes you sneeze or get itchy red eyes, but rather a protein that is produced in the cat's saliva and glands in the skin. Normally, cats lick their fur and spread this protein to their hair. It is also carried on dander, flakes of dead skin that cats continually shed (like the dandruff from people's scalps). While sphynx do not shed hair like other cats, they do have dander. But some people with only mild allergies may be able to live with a sphynx without the allergy symptons another cat breed would cause.

ORIGIN OF THE SPHYNX

The sphynx first appeared in Toronto, Canada, in 1966, when a black and white pet cat, named Elizabeth, gave birth to a hairless kitten in a litter of shorthairs. The owner named the hairless kitten Prune because of his wrinkly, naked body. Prune and his mother were bought by breeders Ridyadh and Yania Bawa, who wanted to use them in a new breeding program. When Prune was old enough, he was mated back to his mother to produce more hairless kittens. At first, this new breed was called the Canadian hairless. In the 1970s, the breed was renamed sphinx (later changed to sphynx) because people thought the cats looked like ancient Egyptian cat sculptures. Actually, a sphynx cat doesn't really look like an

Egyptian sphinx, which had a heavy, muscular body and the head of a human pharaoh. The statues it resembles are images of the cat goddess, Bastet.

The breeding program produced a line of hairless cats that was soon recognized as a new breed by the Cat Fanciers' Association (CFA). However, many of the kittens had health problems, and the CFA withdrew its recognition in 1971. It looked as though the sphynx breed might be doomed, but in 1975 a straight-haired cat named Jezabelle gave birth to a female hairless kitten, Epidermis, on a farm in Wadena, Minnesota. The following year, Jezabelle produced Dermis, another hairless female. Kim Mueske, an Oregon breeder, used these two cats in a breeding program and produced a successful line of sphynx cats.

Meanwhile, in 1978, Shirley Smith, a Toronto breeder, found three hairless kittens (a male and two females) wandering the streets near her home. Ms. Smith sent the two females, Punkie and Paloma, to Dr. Hugo Hernandez, a breeder in the Netherlands, who bred them to a white Devon rex and produced another line of a new sphynx breed. (Remember, Devon rex cats have ultra-short coats.) Through careful breeding, health problems were no longer a major concern. In February 1998, the CFA finally accepted the sphynx again for registration and competition. Crosses with Devon rex and the American shorthair have helped to increase the sphynx population.

SPHYNX CATS AS PETS

The sphynx is a medium-sized cat with a strong, muscular build. Its long neck and long, slender legs resemble those of the extreme Siamese, but its legs are much more muscular. The fine down hairs that cover its body are so small and light-colored that this cat looks hairless. The sphynx's skin is wrinkled, but it doesn't really have more wrinkles than other cat breeds—in other cats the wrinkles don't show because they are covered by the cat's furry coat. Without an insulating coat, the sphynx's body feels warm; its body temperature is at least four degrees higher than that of other cats. A sphynx may have short, curly whiskers or no whiskers at all.

The sphynx comes in a variety of colors and color patterns. Normally, colors appear on a cat's furry coat, but the sphynx's colors show up on its skin. Some of the colors may include white, black, red, brown, calico, and tortoiseshell. They may appear in patches on the body.

The sphynx is one of the sweetest, most lovable of all cat breeds. This cat is very people-oriented, and it also gets along quite well with other pets in the household. The sphynx is very smart and curious and loves to investigate things of interest. This cat will follow you around the house to see what you are doing.

The sphynx is very adventurous and a little mischievous. This active cat may dash around the house without regard to breakable items in the way. It may then give a look as if to say, "Who, me? What did I do?" It's a good idea to put away any breakables when there's a sphynx in the house! Yet this bundle of energy enjoys a nice, cozy nap in its owner's lap or some other warm spot. Without a coat, the cat has little protection against cold and hot temperatures, so keep your sphynx pet indoors.

Even a Hairless Cat Needs Grooming

A Sphynx doesn't have much hair to groom, but this cat is definitely not maintenance-free. Normally, cats produce oils in their skin, which are absorbed by the fur. Without a coat, the Sphynx cannot get rid of these oils. Eventually, they build up and cause skin problems. Therefore, it is very important to wash the Sphynx's skin regularly to remove the oils. Cats that are bathed as kittens are calmer about being washed as adults. To make it easier for the cat, you can use a washcloth rather than putting it in the tub.

INTERNET RESOURCES

www.cfainc.org/breeds/profiles/sphynx.html "CFA Breed Profile: Sphynx"

www.fortunecity.com/greenfield/dreams/383/sphynx.htm "Sphynx"

www.i-love-cats.com/Breeds/sphynx.htm "Cat Breed Descriptions: Sphynx"

www.thecatsite.com/breeds/sphynx.html "The Sphynx Cat"

www.hairlesscats.com/About_the_Sphynx.html "Purrsonality of the Sphynx"

www.apophis.com/faq.htm "Frequently Asked Questions About Sphynx Cats"

FAST FACTS

Scientific name	*Caracal caracal* in Family Felidae, Order Carnivora
Cost	About $1,800 to $2,000
Food	Commercial cat food lacks important nutrients these cats need. Some breeders recommend a special canned food for exotic cats called ZuPre-em. Others say their diet should also include raw chicken (including the bones).
Housing	Should be kept indoors, if possible. Remove all breakable objects. Nothing is safe, not even on a high shelf. Should have cat toys to keep the animal busy and entertained. An outdoor run must be *completely* enclosed, including a fenced roof.
Training	Training requires patience. They may be trained to use a litter box, but not as easily as domestic cats. They should be trained to walk on a leash at a very young age. They may also learn to do tricks, such as jumping up to catch toys or retrieving a toy. Treats are helpful in teaching tricks.
Special notes	Check with your local authorities before getting a pet serval or caracal. Special permits may be needed. For safety, these cats must be declawed on all four paws.

THE CARACAL

THE CARACAL

WOULD YOU LIKE TO have a leopard, a tiger, or a cougar for a pet? They look really cool, and they're fun to watch. But these big cats would not make good pets. They are completely wild, and it could be very dangerous to own one. There are some exotic cats, however, that people can keep as pets. One of these exotic pets is the caracal. Caracals can be tamed, but they are not domesticated. Even though they may be sweet and lovable to their owners, their wild instincts are still strong.

> ### Big Cats vs. Little Cats
>
> *Lions, tigers, leopards, and jaguars are the big cats of the cat family. They belong to a different group than the smaller cats such as the bobcat, lynx, serval, caracal, and domestic cats. The big cats are sometimes called the "roaring cats" because they have a special sound-making structure that allows them to produce a thunderous roar. Smaller cats do not have the ability to roar. All cats, big and small, can purr when they are feeling happy and content.*

Owning an exotic animal sounds exciting, but it is a big responsibility. An exotic cat requires a lot more work and attention than owning a domesticated house cat. So if you are interested in keeping an exotic cat as a pet, make sure you do plenty of research, and be aware of what you are getting yourself into before you make this life-changing decision.

LIFE IN THE WILD

Understanding a cat's life in the wild can help you understand its behavior when you take it into your home. The caracal comes from Asia and Africa, living in dry areas such as woodlands, savannahs, mountains, and stony scrub. Caracals prowl mainly at night, stalking birds, small mammals, lizards, and insects; they also eat some plant leaves and fruits. A caracal can jump up to catch a bird in flight, knocking it down with its paws. It is good at climbing trees and may take its catch

43

up into a tree to eat, to avoid being bothered by other predators. Caracals are the fastest runners among cats of their size, with lightning-quick reflexes. They sometimes attack young goats and other livestock and may kill more animals than they need to eat.

In the wild, each caracal has its own home range, where it hunts and sleeps. Caracals get together only at mating times, when males from miles around are attracted by the female's scent.

CARACALS AS PETS

The caracal is larger than the average domestic cat, weighing between 20 and 40 pounds (9 to 18 kilograms). Its coat color is typical of wild mammals—cream, tan, or orange. Its large ears have distinctive black tufts, making it look very much like a lynx. (The name *caracal* comes from a Turkish word meaning "black ears.") All-black forms have been found in the wild.

One of the main reasons that caracals are suitable as pets, while most other wild cat species are not, is that they are easily tamed and become very affectionate. In buying a caracal, it is important to deal with an experienced breeder who provides a lot of hands-on contact with the animals from a very young age. Plenty of early human contact helps to make these exotic cats calmer.

Just like domestic cats, caracals love to play. They are natural retrievers and enjoy playing fetch. However, when playing with a pet caracal, remember that these cats are still wild by nature. If they get carried away, they can cause a lot of damage or even hurt someone. For this reason, pet caracals should be declawed—on all four paws! Unlike the light scratches you may get from a domestic cat, a scratch from a caracal could send you to the hospital.

You should never let a pet caracal outside on the loose. They are excitable and could hurt neighbors or their pets. Even a fenced-in area is not good enough to hold these cats, since they are such good jumpers. An outdoor enclosure should be covered by a fenced roof. If you want to take your pet outside with you, start training it very early to walk on a leash.

Caracals usually get along with other pets, such as domestic cats or dogs. They may get a little rough when playing with domestic cats, though. Keeping pet rodents or birds in the same home as a caracal is not a good idea since it will consider them as prey.

Although caracals live an average of six years in the wild, they may live as long as eighteen or nineteen years when kept as pets.

The Serval

Let's take a look at another exotic pet choice: the serval. Servals look rather like small cheetahs, with long legs and a slim, muscular body built for running. Their cream or tan coat has rows of dark brown or black spots on the sides and stripes down the back. These medium-sized cats are found over most of Africa, especially in the grassy savannahs and the nearby woodlands and thickets; but unlike caracals, servals like areas near rivers or streams. Fish and amphibians make up a good part of their diet. Servals also use their long front paws to reach into a burrow and snag a rodent hiding inside. They hunt mainly by sound, picking up the tiny noises of scurrying rodents with their antennalike ears. They slink through the thick vegetation and then rise on their hind legs to pounce on their prey. Servals are good jumpers, too—they can jump as high as 12 feet (close to 4 meters) from a standstill. They are normally solitary animals, living alone except at mating times. But if small prey is scarce, two or three servals may team up to catch larger animals, such as antelope.

Servals are easily tamed. Egyptians kept them as pets thousands of years ago. They have been popular pets in Europe for several hundred years but did not become popular in the United States until the twentieth century. These cats are affectionate and playful. A serval likes to stick its long front paws into people's pockets to see if it can "fish out" anything interesting. It also likes to fish for toys in a tub of water. But for safety, it must be declawed and can be allowed outdoors only on a leash or in a fenced enclosure with a roof.

INTERNET RESOURCES

www.rzu2u.com/caracal.htm "Caracal"

www.scz.org/animals/c/caracal.html "Caracal"

ds.dial.pipex.com/agarman/bco/caracal.htm "Caracal"

www.fortunecity.com/greenfield/dreams/383/Wild%20Cats/caracal.htm "Caracal"

www15.brinkster.com/efexotics/caracaltext.html "Caracal"

www.patzmeow.com/africanserval.html "The African Serval Cat"

www.primenet.com/~brendel/serval.html "Servals (Leptailurus serval)"

www.htcirclecexotics.com/servals.htm "Serval (Felis Serval)"

www.vanislefelines.com/servals/interest.html "Vanisle Servals FAQ"

www.rzu2u.com/serval.htm "Serval"

www.patzmeow.com/africanservalcare.html "Care Information for African Servals"

www.valleystables-exotics.com/serval.htm "The African Serval Cat"

www.valleystables-exotics.com/serval1.htm#2 "Serval Cat FAQ"

NOT A PET!

A FRIEND OF OURS used to work in an animal hospital and once spent a fascinating month raising an orphaned Florida panther kitten. She and her mother took turns getting up several times each night to feed Elsie, the kitten, bottles of a special milk formula for cats and caring for her during the day. The kitten grew quickly and soon was able to eat baby food; when she graduated to "real" meat, she was returned to her owners at a small private zoo. Elsie was a beautiful animal, but there was never any thought that she would become a house pet. Florida panthers, related to cougars and mountain lions, are big cats as adults, and though Elsie received a lot of hands-on, loving contact with humans, she was never fully tamed. Like the other big cats, she would have been much too dangerous a pet.

If you've come home from a circus or zoo dreaming of owning a big cat someday, forget it. Lions, tigers, leopards, and cheetahs are beautiful animals, but only trained professionals can handle them—and even zookeepers and circus animal trainers are sometimes badly injured. Some wildcat species are endangered, too. Their numbers are so small that capturing some for the pet trade might lower the species' chances for survival. So if you have a passion for wild animals, volunteer at a zoo or wildlife rehabilitation center. If you just like the "wild look," get a Bengal cat or an ocicat (an all-domestic breed that looks like a miniature ocelot). And if you just love cats, there are plenty of them in animal shelters that could use some tender, loving, volunteer care. Perhaps you might wind up taking one home.

Is a cat the right pet for you? If you are looking for a pet that will give you unquestioning loyalty and devotion, one that can be taught to obey your every command, then maybe you'd be better off with a dog. A pet cat can learn to love you, adores being petted, and may follow you around or come to investigate what you are doing and sit on your lap (or on the book you are trying to read). But it shows its affection when it is in the mood, and sometimes it is not. Cats are more independent than dogs, and the ease of training them to use a litter box is convenient. But the final choice often comes down to your inner feelings. It is a choice that should not be made lightly or hastily—when well cared for, a cat or dog may live for ten, fifteen, or even twenty years. Owning a pet is a long-term responsibility, one that, sadly, many people do not take seriously enough. Each year, six million unwanted animals (mostly cats and dogs) are destroyed at animal shelters!

Should you get a purebred cat? The breeds differ mainly in appearance, although some breeds have typical personalities. Siamese are usually very talkative and active, for example, while Persians are more laid-back. Reputable breeders are the best sources for purebred cats.

Purebred animals can be very expensive, and unless you want your cat to compete at cat shows, you will probably be just as happy with a mixed-breed cat. Adopting a cat or kitten from an animal shelter may save its life. At the better-run shelters, the workers spend a lot of time getting kittens socialized and helping older cats to work through any hang-ups left by their previous experiences. You may even find purebred cats at a shelter. Breeders may also have some "pet quality" animals for sale—cats that do not meet the rigid breed standards but can be playful and loving pets.

FOR FURTHER INFORMATION

Note: Before attempting to keep a kind of pet that is new to you, it is a good idea to read one or more pet manuals about that species or breed. Check your local library, pet shop, or bookstore. Search for information on the species or breed on the Internet.

BOOKS

Birr, Uschi. *Beautiful Cats: The Most Popular Breeds.* New York: Sterling Publishing Co., 1998.

Cutts, Paddy. *Illustrated Encyclopedia: Cat Breeds of the World.* New York: Lorenz Books, 1999.

Edwards, Alan, and Grace McHattie. *The Big Book of Cats.* Philadelphia: Courage Books, 1999.

Fogle, Bruce. *The Encyclopedia of the Cat.* New York: Dorling Kindersley, 1997.

Morris, Desmond. *Cat Breeds of the World.* New York: Viking, 1999.

Richards, James R. *ASPCA Complete Guide to Cats.* San Francisco: Chronicle Books, 1999.

Spadafori, Gina, and Paul D. Pion. *Cats for Dummies.* Foster City, CA: IDG Books, 1997.

INTERNET RESOURCES

www.acfacat.com/ "American Cat Fanciers' Association"

www.aspca.org/ "ASPCA: The American Society for the Prevention of Cruelty to Animals"

www.cfainc.org/ "The Cat Fanciers' Association"

www.pawprintonline.com/central-b4ubuy.html "Before You Buy"

www.petfinder.org/ "Petfinder"

www.tica.org/ "The International Cat Association"

PERIODICALS

Cat Fancy (monthly); *Cats & Kittens* (bimonthly); *Cats Magazine* (monthly); *I Love Cats Magazine* (bimonthly)

INDEX

Page numbers in *italics* refer to illustrations.